Kiss the Crocodile

Sean Taylor and Ben Mantle

WALKER BOOKS
AND SUBSIDIARIES
LONDON · BOSTON · SYDNEY · AUCKLAND

Look at the fun these three are having.
"I know a game!" says Monkey.
"Let's all play ... STICK SPLASH!"

PLISH!

PLASH!

PLOSH!

Anteater says, "I know another game!
Let's all play ... SCARY MONSTERS!"

GAAARGH!

WAAARGH!

YAAARGH!

Tortoise says, "Let's all play **SILLY DANCING** now!"

Monkey's dance is *so* silly, she almost falls in the mud-hole and ...

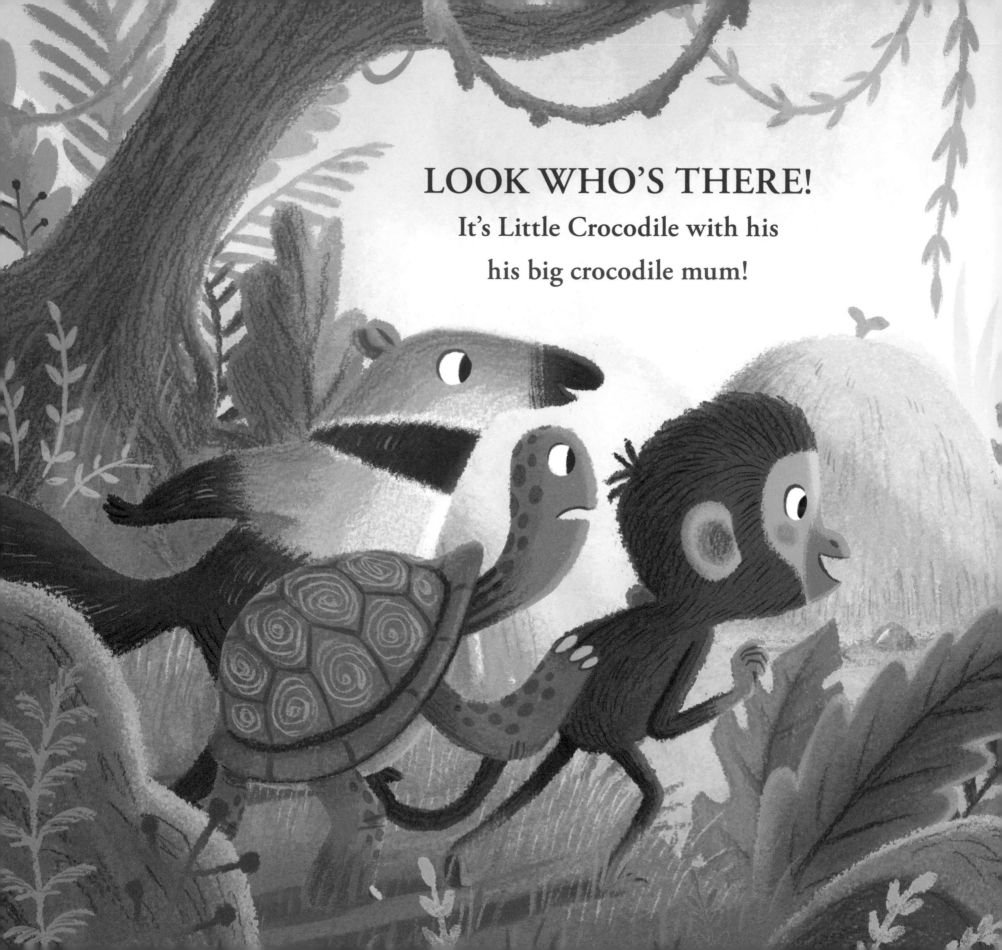

LOOK WHO'S THERE!

It's Little Crocodile with his

his big crocodile mum!

Anteater whispers, "Those are *sharp* claws!"
Tortoise whispers, "What a *lot* of teeth!"
Monkey whispers, "LET'S KEEP BACK!"

But Little Crocodile spots them.

His mum says, "You can play
a game we like, if you want...
It's called KISS THE CROCODILE!"

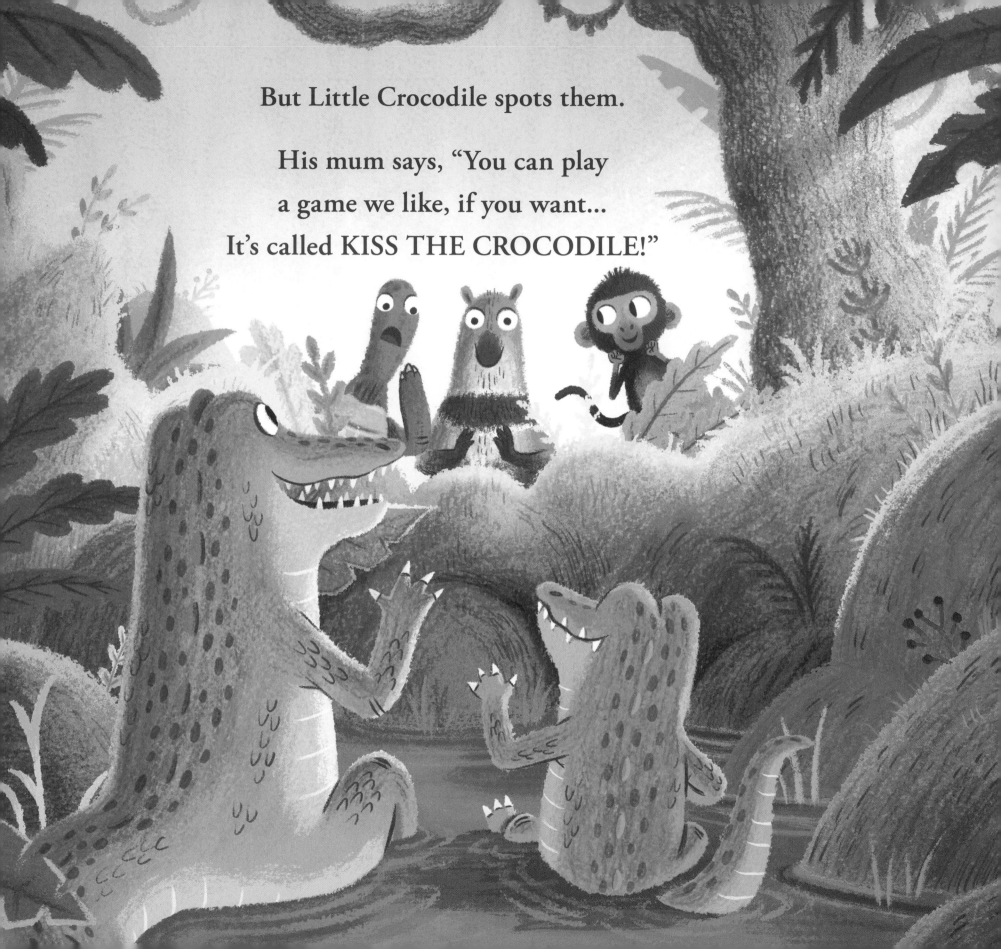

Little Crocodile really wants them to play.

He says, "I lie here, asleep.

And you mustn't wake me up!

But you have to be brave enough to

KISS THE CROCODILE!"

Monkey says, "OK! I'm brave enough!"

"I bet I can actually be brave enough first!" says Anteater.

"I bet maybe you CAN'T!" says Monkey.

But Anteater checks to make sure Little Crocodile looks asleep.

Then she tip-toes over,
ever so very quietly.

She reaches down,
even more ever so
very quietly and ...

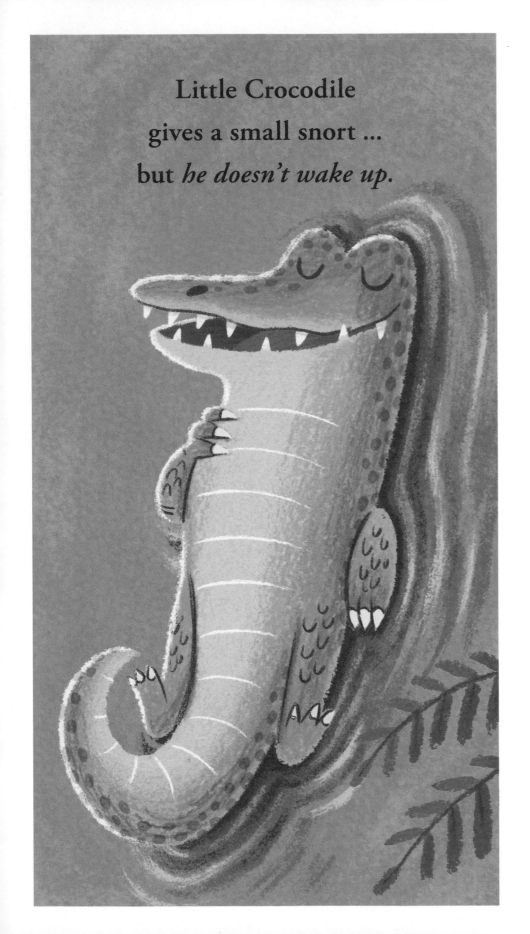

Little Crocodile
gives a small snort ...
but *he doesn't wake up.*

Anteater asks,
"Who's brave enough to
KISS THE CROCODILE next?"

Tortoise thinks.
Then he says,
"ME."

He checks to make sure
Little Crocodile still looks
asleep. He walks over
very, very, very,
very slowly.

He reaches his lips up
even more very, very,
very, *very* slowly and ...

KISSES THE CROCODILE!

SMOOOCH!

Little Crocodile
moves an eyelid ...
but he *doesn't wake up*.

Tortoise says,
"How about you, Monkey?"
"OK," says Monkey.

But ... she doesn't move.
"You said you were brave
enough," Anteater tells her.
"I know," says Monkey.

"It's only a game!"
whispers Anteater.
And Tortoise says,
"KISS THE CROCODILE!"

And she goes ...
a little bit ...
but then she comes back!

So Monkey scampers quickly across.

She swings down in a hurry and ...

KISSES THE CROCODILE!

SMACK!

And Little Crocodile ...

Monkey skids
and scurries!

But Little Crocodile skids
and scurries faster!

So Monkey turns around. And she says,
"We were only playing the game you like!
What happens NOW?"

And Little Crocodile says,
"NOW, can I play a game *you* like?"

So he does.

And look at the fun *these four* are having...
They play STICK SPLASH.
And guess who makes the biggest splash?

PLOOOSH!

They play SCARY MONSTERS.

And guess who's the scariest?

NYAK
NYAK
NYAK!

Then ...
Little Crocodile says,
"I know another game.
Let's all play ...

KISS THE
MONKEY!"

"All right," Monkey laughs.
"If you're *brave* enough!"

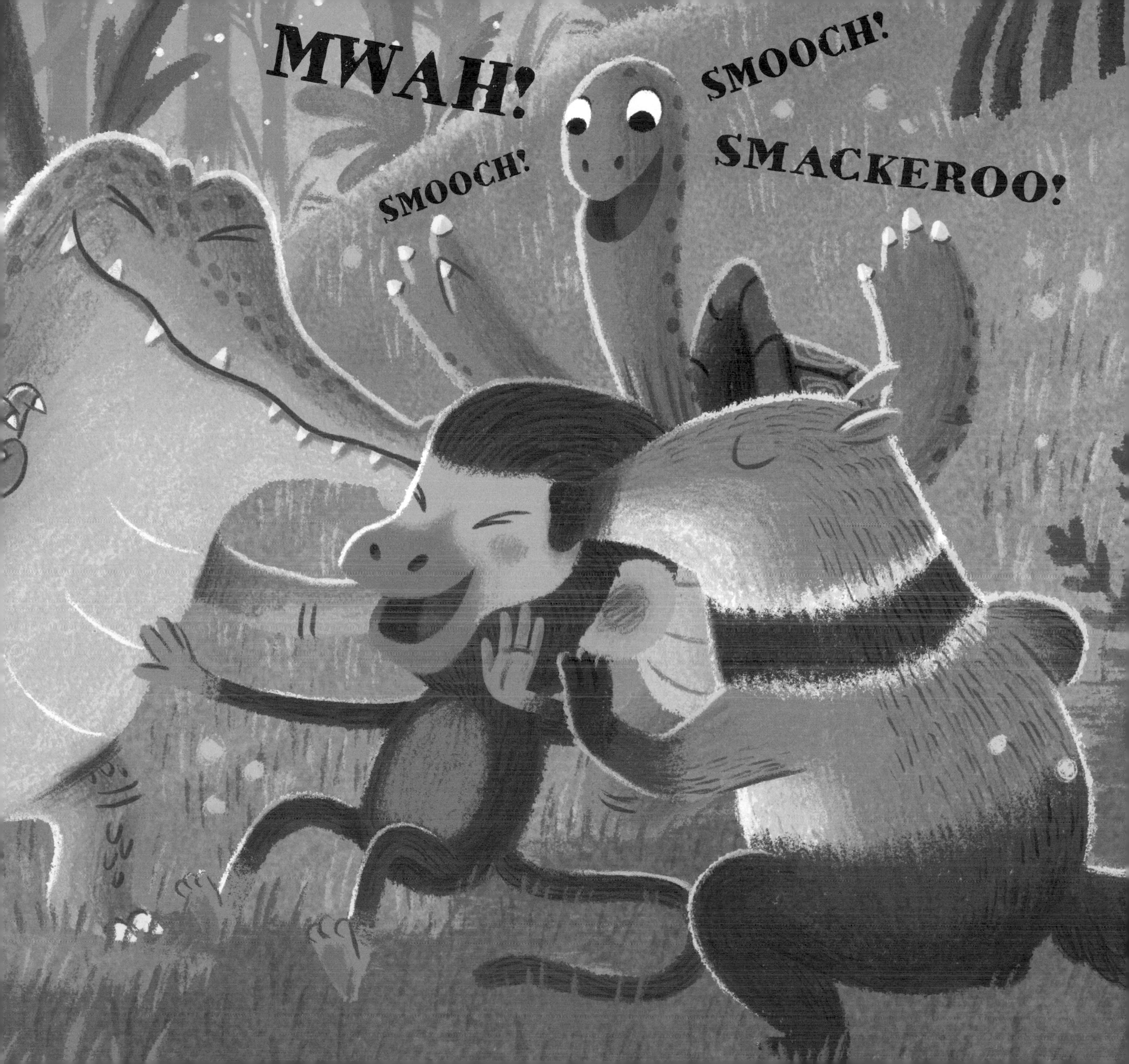
MWAH!
SMOOCH!
SMOOCH!
SMACKEROO!

Para Raul ~ S.T.

For Ella May Harrison ~ B.M.

First published 2019 by Walker Books Ltd, 87 Vauxhall Walk, London SE11 5HJ • Text © 2019 Sean Taylor • Illustrations © 2019 Ben Mantle • The right of Sean Taylor and Ben Mantle to be identified as author and illustrator of this work has been asserted by them in accordance with the Copyright, Designs and Patents Act 1988 • This book has been typeset in Adobe Garamond Pro • Printed in Italy • All rights reserved. No part of this book may be reproduced, transmitted or stored in an information retrieval system in any form or by any means, graphic, electronic or mechanical, including photocopying, taping and recording, without prior written permission from the publisher • British Library Cataloguing in Publication Data: a catalogue record for this book is available from the British Library • ISBN 978-1-4063-6934-2 (hb) • 978-1-4063-8792-6 (pb) • www.walker.co.uk • 10 9 8 7 6 5 4 3 2 1